Sugar Plum Ballerinas

Dancing Diva

Sugar Plum Ballerinas

WHOOPI GOLDBERG

Sugar Plum Ballerinas

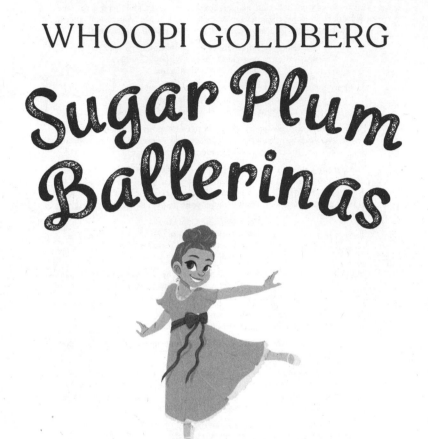

Dancing Diva

with Deborah Underwood
Illustrated by Ashley Evans

LITTLE, BROWN AND COMPANY
New York Boston

Text copyright © 2012 by Whoopi Goldberg
Illustrations copyright © 2023 by Whoopi Goldberg
Illustrations by Ashley Evans

Cover art copyright © 2023 by Whoopi Goldberg. Cover art by Ashley Evans.
Cover design by Sasha Illingworth.
Cover copyright © 2023 by Hachette Book Group, Inc.

Little, Brown and Company
Hachette Book Group
1290 Avenue of the Americas, New York, NY 10104
Visit us at LBYR.com

Originally published in hardcover and paperback by Disney • Jump at the Sun Books, an imprint of Disney Book Group, in May 2012
Revised Trade Paperback Edition: January 2023

Little, Brown and Company is a division of Hachette Book Group, Inc. The Little, Brown name and logo are trademarks of Hachette Book Group, Inc.

The publisher is not responsible for websites (or their content) that are not owned by the publisher.

Little, Brown and Company books may be purchased in bulk for business, educational, or promotional use. For information, please contact your local bookseller or the Hachette Book Group Special Markets Department at special.markets@hbgusa.com.

Library of Congress Cataloging-in-Publication Data
Names: Goldberg, Whoopi, 1955– author. | Underwood, Deborah, author. |
Evans, Ashley, illustrator.
Title: Dancing diva / Whoopi Goldberg with Deborah Underwood ;
illustrated by Ashley Evans.
Description: Revised trade paperback edition. | New York : Little, Brown and Company,
2023. | Series: Sugar Plum ballerinas | Audience: Ages 6–10. | Summary: When Epatha
tries to spice up the choreography of the new ballet in Harlem with her free-spirited
style, the rest of the Sugar Plum ballerinas encourage her to keep her toes in line.
Identifiers: LCCN 2022013923 | ISBN 9780316295017 (trade paperback) |
ISBN 9781423154662 (ebook)
Subjects: CYAC: Ballet dancing—Fiction. | African Americans—Fiction. |
Harlem (New York, N.Y.)—Fiction.
Classification: LCC PZ7.G56443 Dan 2023 | DDC [Fic]—dc23
LC record available at https://lccn.loc.gov/2022013923

ISBNs: 978-0-316-29501-7 (pbk.), 978-1-4231-5466-2 (ebook)

Printed in the United States of America

LSC-C

Printing 1, 2022

To anyone with a dream

CHAPTER

1

"EPATHA!"

"I'm in the kitchen, Abuela," I say. I'm standing at the sink, where a big plastic dishpan full of bright purple dye is waiting. I carefully examine my old spaghetti-sauce-stained leotard. (When your parents own an Italian restaurant, a lot of your clothes end up with spaghetti-sauce stains.) I'll start with the sleeves, then see what happens.

I dip the edge of the leotard into the dye and smile as the purple creeps up into the fabric. Then I dip the other sleeve in. But finally I can't help myself: I push the whole thing into the pan. The dye water feels nice and warm, even through the rubber gloves I'm wearing.

I lift the leotard out. Where it was crumpled up, there are streaks of white that make cool patterns. But mostly it's purple, purple, purple. *¡Fabuloso!*

Abuela appears in the doorway. "Another creation, Epatha? *Precioso.*" She leans closer and whispers, "I think you get this flair for bold colors from me. Not from Nonna."

As if on cue, Nonna, my other grandmother, comes into the kitchen. She is as short and stout as Abuela is lean and graceful.

As usual, she's wearing all black. She waddles over to the sink.

"*Bello*, Epatha. Very nice. *Colori vivi brillanti*—but wearing bright colors is just fine. For children," she says, glancing at Abuela's flaming-red pantsuit.

Here we go again. Nonna is my dad's mom. When my grandpa died, she moved from Italy to live with us. I was just a baby then, so she's been here as long as I can remember. Abuela is Mom's mom. She moved here from Puerto Rico a year ago, and I think

Nonna's still mad about it. They're always bickering about something.

"After you clean up, maybe you'd like some *mantecaditos*," Abuela says. *Mantecaditos* are Puerto Rican butter cookies, one of Abuela's specialties.

"Hmph," Nonna grunts. "I think she would rather have some of my biscotti. And you don't need to clean up, *cara mia*. You have had a busy day at school. Go, relax. I will bring you a snack."

"I still need to rinse this out," I say, holding up the leotard, which is dripping purple dye into the sink.

"I will rinse, I will rinse," Nonna says. "Go." She pushes me away from the sink, I guess so she can start rinsing before Abuela decides *she'll* clean up after me. But Abuela's already at the kitchen cabinet loading up a plate with cookies she baked this morning.

I shrug. It makes them happy to do things for me, and to tell the truth, I hate cleaning up dye—it makes a big mess. So I carefully peel off my gloves and head to my room. I know that in five minutes, both grandmas will be at my door with heaping plates of cookies. I'll eat exactly the same number of

4

each. I made the mistake of eating more of Abuela's once, and Nonna stomped around in a huff for days. Then, when they're not looking, I'll stick the rest of the cookies in my sock drawer until I can smuggle them out to my friends.

As I head down the hallway to my room, I remember I left my backpack downstairs in our restaurant.

When I walk through the swinging doors at the bottom of the stairs and into the restaurant kitchen, a blast of warm, garlic-scented air hits my face. One of the kitchen guys is unloading the dishwasher. The sound of clattering silverware echoes off the shiny walls.

Bella Italia is almost empty, which isn't unusual for this time of day; it's only four thirty in the afternoon, and the dinner crowd won't start drifting in for another hour or so. Mom and Dad are talking quietly in a booth. This freaks me out a little. I'm trying to think of the last time I saw both of them sitting down in the restaurant. Usually they're *doing* something: filling salt shakers, straightening napkins on the tables, or sweeping up after a toddler has decided to toss sugar packets all over the floor.

"It won't be easy," Dad says. "How will she get to all those rehearsals if she gets in?"

"We can figure it out," Mom says. "Amarah can help, now that she's in college. Most of her classes meet before noon. And it would be too bad for Epatha to miss out just because of logistics."

"What are logistics?" I ask. "What are you talking about?"

They both jump up. "Nothing, *querida*," Mom says.

"What *kind* of nothing?" I ask.

"Don't worry—it's a good nothing," Mom says. "You'll find out tomorrow at your ballet class."

Dad bolts for the kitchen, and Mom rushes after him. I'm left in the empty room with my mouth hanging open.

CHAPTER
2

THE NEXT AFTERNOON, I BOUND UP THE STAIRS OF THE Nutcracker School. It's a gorgeous April day. The trees are just starting to get tiny pink buds on their branches. For the first time this year, I'm not wearing my winter coat. I look *fabulosa* in my new purple leotard, and I can't wait for everyone to see it. And more importantly, I'm dying to know more about the good nothing.

My friends are gathered in our usual corner of the waiting room. Terrel, Brenda, and one of the triplets—Jerzey Mae—are clumped together talking as they put on their ballet slippers. Terrel offers

everyone White Rabbit candies. Terrel's dad is Chinese American, and whenever he buys the popular Chinese candies, Terrel brings some to class. Jessica, another triplet, is scribbling on a piece of paper. Al and JoAnn, the third triplet, are looking at a skateboard website. Since JoAnn recently broke her leg on a skateboard, this surprises me.

"Don't tell me you're getting back on a skateboard," I say, dropping my dance bag on the bench. "*Ragazza pazza.* You're wild, girlfriend."

"I busted my leg because I *tripped* on my skateboard. In my *room*. Not because I was riding it,"

JoAnn says, with exag-
gerated patience. I get the
feeling she's said this a few
times before. Probably to
her parents.

"When she actually
rides a skateboard, she
wears knee pads and a helmet and stuff," Al adds.

"Maybe you need to wear knee pads and a helmet
walking around your room," I say.

"Not a bad idea," JoAnn admits. Of the triplets'
rooms, hers is always the messiest.

Jessica glances up from her paper. She looks me up and down. "Is that leotard new?" she asks. "It's a beautiful color."

I proudly turn around, displaying my fabulous, newly purple creation. "Yes," I say. "Fresh from Epatha's House of Dyeing."

Jerzey Mae's eyes widen. "Who's dying? Is it contagious?"

Brenda shakes her head. "Hypochondriac a such are you." Brenda talks backward a lot of the time. We can understand her, but grown-ups can't, which sometimes comes in very handy.

"What's a hypochondriac?" Jerzey Mae asks, alarmed.

"Someone who thinks she's getting sick all the time," says Terrel. "Like you." She puts her sneakers neatly under the bench.

"Not *dying* dying, Jerzey Mae. I meant fabric dyeing," I say impatiently, eager to get everyone's attention back on my new creation. "Do you like the white streaks?"

"Nice," Terrel says. "But couldn't you get them to go in a straight line? They're kind of all over the place."

I exhale. "They're not *supposed* to go in a straight line, T.," I say. "They're creative! They go wherever they want to! That's the beauty of tie-dye. Straight lines are boring."

I sit down on the bench beside Jessica.

"Whatcha doing?"

"She's writing a poem," Jerzey Mae says. "A sonnet."

"A what?"

Jessica looks up. "A sonnet. It's a kind of poem that has fourteen lines." She starts talking about the rhyme scheme—something about *A*'s and *B*'s and *C*'s—but I'm stuck on the fourteen-line business.

"Why does it have to have fourteen lines?" I say.

Jessica shrugs. "It just does. That's what a sonnet is: a fourteen-line poem."

This sounds silly to me. "But what if you've got more than fourteen lines to say? Or less than fourteen lines?"

Jessica laughs. "That's just the way it works, E. When you write sonnets, you're supposed to be creative inside the rules you're given."

I snort. "Creativity and rules don't go together."

"Tell that to Shakespeare," Jessica says.

"Your rat? Why would I talk to your rat?" Shakespeare, Jessica's white rat, once made a visit to the Nutcracker School, when the triplets' little brother, Mason, snuck him into class, but now he's home in his cage. I hope.

"Not the rat. Shakespeare the playwright and poet, the man that Shakespeare the rat is named after," Jessica says. "He wrote over a hundred sonnets, and they're plenty creative."

I'm about to tell her that they'd probably have been *more* creative if they had had interesting numbers of lines, like seventeen or nine or forty-seven. But just then, the waiting room door opens, and our teacher, Ms. Debbé, comes in. She always dresses in a very creative way, and today is no exception. She's all in bright blue, from the top of her turban to the tips of her shiny boots. Her son, Mr. Lester, stands beside her.

"What's he doing here?" Terrel whispers. Mr. Lester teaches some classes at our school, but he usually doesn't teach us. He spends a lot of his time working at the Harlem Ballet. When Ms. Debbé was a dancer, she danced with the Harlem Ballet. I'll bet she thinks it's cool that now her son is a director there.

Then it dawns on me. The *nothing*! I'll bet Mr. Lester knows what it is—and I'll bet we're about to find out.

CHAPTER
3

"THERE'S SOME BIG BALLET SECRET!" I WHISPER TO TERREL. "I heard Mom and Dad talking about it. They said we'll find out today, and—"

Thump thump thump. Ms. Debbé taps her walking stick on the floor. "The class, it begins," she says, her French accent thick as ever. She turns gracefully and heads for the studio. Mr. Lester follows her.

We drift to the doorway and clomp up the old wooden stairs. Once inside the studio, we go straight to the barre. Mr. Lester sits on a folding chair in a back corner of the room while Ms. Debbé leads us through our warm-up exercises. This is strange at first, but after a while I forget he's there.

"Demi-plié! Grand plié! Demi-plié! And up!" calls Ms. Debbé.

I stand at the barre between Terrel and Jerzey Mae, who's gotten so much better over the past year that I can hardly believe it. She's just as good as anyone in the class now, although every once in a while she slips back into being old Jerzey Mae, turning the wrong way and crashing into one of us.

Even though Terrel's a year younger than the rest of us, she's a really good dancer. When we turn to face in the other direction, her pivot is neat and clear—no wasted movement, nothing out of place. If you saw Terrel do a hundred pliés, they'd all look exactly the same.

That's not how *I* dance. To me, dance is about being creative. You can't do creative things with your legs while you're pliéing, but you can do all sorts of stuff with your arms. You can hold them out straight, or add little swirly movements, or swoop them around like you're a falcon flying through the air.

"Not so wild, Epatha," says Ms. Debbé. "We are doing graceful pliés, not flapping our wings."

She knew I was being a bird—excellent! But I try to do what she says, and for the next few pliés, I imagine my arms are as soft and gentle as dandelion fluff.

Just as I get itchy to try something else, we move on to battement tendus, where you slide your foot on the floor and point your toe. You're supposed to slide it straight forward, then straight to the side, then straight back. But I think it's more interesting to trace squiggles on the floor. As I go to the side, I imagine that my foot is a fish riding on an ocean wave. Up, down, up, down…

"Epatha!" Ms. Debbé calls. "Straight and precise, please."

Needless to say, Terrel's tendus are straight and precise. "Don't you get tired of doing the same thing over and over?" I whisper to her while Ms. Debbé is correcting a girl at the other end of the barre.

"Don't you get tired of having Ms. Debbé yell at you?" she says.

"But doing the same thing is—"

"Epatha!" Ms. Debbé calls. "Concentrate, please."

Terrel may have a point.

Class goes quickly, and soon it's almost over. I expect Ms. Debbé to start working with us on some new dances, but instead she asks us to sit on the floor. Mr. Lester joins her at the front of the room. He's holding a stack of papers.

"Now. There are a few exciting things," Ms. Debbé says. "First, I want to tell you again that you did a wonderful show last week."

Everyone claps, and I high-five each of my friends. Last week was major drama—we thought the ballet school was going to close, but, thanks to a cat that Jessica smuggled in to the school, we found a nesting peregrine falcon on the roof and had a big benefit concert that raised tons of money. It's kind of a long story.

"But it seems," Ms. Debbé continues, "that there is more excitement in store for some of you. I will let Mr. Lester tell you about it." She moves off to the side of the room.

Mr. Lester starts right in. "I've already told your parents about this, but I asked them not to say anything to you."

Aha—so *this* is the *nothing*! I lean forward eagerly.

Mr. Lester continues, "The Harlem Ballet is premiering a new ballet called *Springtime in Harlem* this May. Most of the roles will be danced by professional dancers, but there are also some parts for girls your age."

Excitement floods my body. "Yeesssss!" I say out loud. Even though I'm sitting down, I do a little victory dance. "We're gonna be ballet stars! We're gonna be ballet stars!" I chant.

Jessica grins.

I don't get in trouble, because the whole room has dissolved into chaos. Mr. Lester claps to get our attention. "As I was saying, there will be parts for a number of girls. There's also a bigger role for one girl."

My hand flies up in the air. "Me! Me!"

Mr. Lester motions for me to put my hand down. "Since this is a professional production, we'll be choosing dancers by audition. After class on Saturday, anyone who wants can stay to learn a short routine. Then the director of the show will decide which dancers will make up the group of girls, and who will get the bigger part."

"Aren't you the director?" Al asks.

Mr. Lester shakes his head. "I'm helping out with this production, but Alfonso Tonetti will direct." He waves the papers he's been holding. "Being in the ballet will require extra rehearsals, and of course you must be there for all the performances. If you want to audition, have your parents fill out this commitment form. You need to bring it back, signed, on Saturday. No exceptions." He begins handing out the forms.

A small, dark-haired girl raises her hand. "I'm not going to be here on Saturday. I have a birthday party to go to."

"I'm sorry," Mr. Lester says. "We're only holding auditions on Saturday. If you're not here then, you're out of luck."

The girl opens and closes her mouth like a fish, but she takes a commitment form anyway. So do all my friends.

A professional ballet! I can just see it now. There I am, in a beautiful costume, dancing under the spotlight. As we finish, the entire theater—and I'll bet the Harlem Ballet theater is pretty big—explodes in applause. People run forward with huge bouquets of flowers for us. I take a solo bow as people cheer and scream...

"Epatha!" Terrel says, sharply.

I look around. The studio is empty. Even our friends have gone.

"Where the heck have you been?" she asks. "Off in la-la land?"

I stand up quickly. "I was just thinking." I run to the side of the room to grab my bag, and then we walk out together. "Are you going to audition?"

"Of course," Terrel says. She doesn't even ask if I'm going to audition. She knows.

I feel bad for a second. Terrel and I are the best dancers in the class. But she dances like a mechanical doll. Everything she does is precise and perfect. But I dance with emotion and feeling, like the dance moves are building up inside me and *have* to come out. I'm sure that a professional ballet company is going to want someone who dances with true feeling for the starring role. That's me. I hope Terrel won't be too disappointed.

CHAPTER
4

THE WEEK SEEMS TO DRAG ON FOREVER, BUT FINALLY SAT-
urday arrives. We have class as usual; and then Ms.
Debbé tells us that anyone who wants to audition
should wait in the studio. She says that Mr. Lester
and Mr. Tonetti have been held up in traffic, but are
on their way.

Only about two-thirds of the class stays, probably because the rehearsal schedule is a bit intense.
That's what I overheard Mom and Dad talking about.
My friends and I are lucky. Our parents can trade off
taking us to rehearsals—that is, if we all get into the
show. I cross my fingers hard.

"How long do you think Mr. Lester and Mr. Tonetti will take to get here?" Jerzey Mae asks, bouncing up and down on one foot as if she has to go to the bathroom.

Al puts her leg up on the barre to stretch. "Who knows?" she says. "I wonder what they're going to make us do for the audition."

Brenda, who has been studying a piece of paper she pulled out of her bag, looks up. "I've been researching auditions online. They'll probably teach us a short routine, then make us do it in small groups, so they can watch us."

Sometimes I can't believe Brenda. "You did research? For an audition?"

"Dancing in a ballet might look good on my college applications," she says matter-of-factly.

Terrel exhales in annoyance. "You're *nine*! How many nine-year-olds are worrying about college applications?"

I want to cut in fast, before Brenda starts telling us that her hero, Leonardo da Vinci, was inventing rocket ships when he was nine or something. But then I notice that Jerzey Mae looks kind of sick. "Are you okay, Jerzey Mae?" I ask.

"She's just nervous," Jessica says. As soon as she hears the word *nervous*, Jerzey Mae clutches her stomach, bends over, and groans.

Brenda snaps into doctor mode.

"Breathe!" she commands, as Jessica pats Jerzey Mae on the back reassuringly.

"Oh, man. She's not gonna throw up, is she?" Al asks, edging away.

"No," Brenda says. "She's going to take some nice deep breaths and calm down. Right, Jerzey Mae?"

Jerzey Mae moans.

Jerzey Mae is the only one bent over in panic, but everyone's a little jumpy. None of us has ever auditioned before.

JoAnn and Al pretend they're not crazy about ballet—JoAnn prefers skateboarding, and Al wants to be a famous speed skater like her idol, Phoebe Fitz—but Jessica told me JoAnn and Al have been practicing ballet in JoAnn's room for the first time. Jessica seems obsessed, as well: she keeps saying over and over that it would be really fun to dance onstage in that big theater.

I glance at Terrel and catch her looking at me, too. We both know that we're each other's competition for the lead part. She is a really good dancer, and it takes a lot to rattle her. But it takes a lot to rattle me, too.

"You or Terrel will get the big part, I bet," Al says, as if she's reading my mind.

I shrug. "Maybe," I say.

Terrel raises an eyebrow.

"You never know what directors will want," I say. I sound convincing. But actually, as far as I'm concerned, that part is already mine.

The studio door opens. The room, which had been filled with nervous conversation, instantly falls silent. Mr. Lester comes in first. He's followed by a short, muscular man in a sports jacket and T-shirt.

"Hello, girls," Mr. Lester says. "I'd like to introduce you to Mr. Tonetti, the director of *Springtime in Harlem*."

Mr. Tonetti glances at us over the top of his black-framed glasses and nods. Frankly, he's a little scary. He's definitely not one of those grown-ups who bend over backward to try to get kids to like him. In fact, he looks like he's not particularly crazy about kids at all.

Mr. Lester pulls a table over from one side of the room. Then he pulls up a couple of folding chairs. Mr. Tonetti immediately sits down and pulls a stack of papers out of his bag.

"Okay, girls," Mr. Lester says. "Sorry to keep you waiting. Let me tell you what's going to happen. I'll teach you a short routine. We'll go over it several times; then, when you've got it down, Mr. Tonetti and I will watch you do it in small groups. Sound good?"

Brenda smiles. Well, fine. So she's good at researching auditions. But they're looking for the best dancers, not the best researchers.

"Any questions before we start?" Mr. Lester asks.

A skinny girl with blond hair and a pink face raises her hand. "How many of us will get to be in the show?"

Mr. Lester and Mr. Tonetti exchange looks. "We're not sure yet," Mr. Lester says. "But it will probably be around six."

Six? That stinks. I really wanted all my friends to be up there dancing with me, but there are seven of us, plus several other girls trying out.

We stand up and move to the center of the dance floor. There are twelve dancers altogether, so we arrange ourselves into four rows of three each. I stand front and center, ready to show Mr. Tonetti what I can do.

"We'll start with a jeté to the left, then one to the right. Then a series of châiné turns, like this." Mr. Lester demonstrates. "Let's try that much. Ready? Three, four, and jeté...two...jeté...four, and turn, two, three, four..."

The routine is pretty easy, and we learn it quickly. I'm glad to see all my friends are doing well. Even Jerzey Mae seems to have overcome her nervousness and is doing all the right steps, in the right directions.

Mr. Lester watches us carefully, giving us some corrections. "Curved left arms here, everyone. Big stretch with your right leg. When you're traveling, be sure to move in straight lines, so you don't get in each other's way."

27

Mr. Tonetti, however, isn't paying the least bit of attention. After he rattles his papers around for a while, he takes out his phone and seems to be reading text messages or e-mails or something. It's a little frustrating. How is he going to see how fabulous I am if he's not even looking at me?

When Mr. Lester is satisfied we've learned the routine, he stops us. "Very nice, ladies. Now we'll have you do it in smaller groups. Let's see.... Martha, Jerzey Mae, and Al, you're in the first group. Everyone else, please take a seat on the side of the room." He sits at the table beside Mr. Tonetti.

The pink-faced girl lines up with Jerzey Mae and Al. Jerzey Mae looks over to us, and Jessica gives her a thumbs-up.

"And...jeté!" Mr. Lester says.

They jump and spin across the floor. Jerzey Mae and Al look great. Martha does pretty well till the very end, when she forgets one of the steps and just stands there.

"Can I do it again?" she says after the group has finished.

"I think we've seen enough," Mr. Lester says. "Very nice."

She looks upset, but I forget about her as I hear Mr. Lester call my name along with Terrel's and Brenda's.

We line up, with me in the center. Brenda looks at me, and I wink. My stomach feels a little jumpy, but now that Mr. Tonetti has put away his phone, I'm eager to dance for him.

"Ready? And...jeté!"

We all jump together, perfectly in unison. My friends and I have performed together a bunch of times, so it's easier dancing with them than it would be with strangers. As always when I'm dancing, it's as if everything I'm feeling—the nervousness, the excitement—gets changed into movement. As we turn, I add in some of my own moves—an arm swirl here, a foot flick there. I want them to know that I'm an original. Not only can I do their routine, I can make it mine!

Before I know it, the routine is over. "Good, girls! JoAnn, Jessica, Terrel, you're up next."

I look over, hoping to see Mr. Tonetti smiling at how great we were, but he's writing notes on one of

his papers. He looks about as excited as someone waiting for a bus. I exhale impatiently.

Terrel, Brenda, and I sit down to watch the other auditions. After everyone has danced, Mr. Lester and Mr. Tonetti whisper to each other. They seem to be arguing about something. Mr. Tonetti glances up at me and whispers some more. Then Mr. Lester looks at me and says something to him in reply. Mr. Tonetti gives me a long, hard glare. It is not the kind of look you give a budding ballet star.

I have a feeling this won't be easy, after all.

CHAPTER
5

FINALLY, MR. LESTER AND MR. TONETTI STOP TALKING. MR. Lester comes over to us. Mr. Tonetti puts his papers back into his bag and takes off, without even saying good-bye.

"You all did a really good job, ladies," Mr. Lester tells us. "Especially since I imagine that for most of you, this was your first audition. They can be pretty nerve-racking, huh?"

Jerzey Mae nods violently.

"I wish we could use all of you in the show, but we've decided that six is the right number for the chorus. We've chosen JoAnn, Jessica, Jerzey Mae, Al, Terrel, and Brenda."

All my friends—but wait a minute. He didn't say my name! My face starts to get hot. This is crazy! I know I danced just as well as they did. Jessica touches my arm, but I pull away from her. It's as if all the air has been sucked out of my lungs, and I've been flattened by a steamroller.

"And the girl we've chosen to have the bigger part..."

Air floods back into my lungs. There's still hope!

"...is Epatha." Yes! JoAnn grins and punches my arm.

Mr. Lester continues, "And Terrel, we'd like you to learn that part as well, so you can be Epatha's understudy. Are you willing to do that?"

Terrel looks over at me a little grudgingly. She nods.

"The rest of you, I'm sorry," Mr. Lester says. Martha's face turns even more red. She picks up her stuff and runs out of the room. The other girls who didn't get parts don't look too happy, either.

"That's it for today, girls," he says. "We'll be learning the dance here and then moving to the theater to start rehearsing there a few weeks before the show. So we'll get started after class Tuesday, yes? See you then."

We all gather our things. "Nice, Epatha!" Al says.

"Yeah—congratulations," JoAnn says. "You did great."

"You guys did, too," I say.

"I'm so glad we're all in the show together!" Jessica says.

Mr. Lester interrupts us. "Epatha, can I see you for a minute?"

"Sure," I say. He must have some special how-to-be-a-big-star tips for me.

"We'll wait for you downstairs," Al says. My friends go out, to the waiting room, leaving Mr. Lester and me alone in the studio.

"Have a seat," he says, rearranging the folding chairs so they face each other.

I sit.

"You did a great job today, Epatha," Mr. Lester says.

I glow.

"Mr. Tonetti and I were both impressed with the energy and the emotion in your dancing."

I knew it! I knew they'd want someone who was an expressive dancer. That's what dancing is all about: showing what's inside you.

He continues, "But—"

There's a *but*? I was fabulous. That's all I want to hear.

"Mr. Tonetti was also concerned that you might not follow the choreography you're given. I know you like to change things up and have a good time when you're dancing—"

"Well, yeah," I interrupt. "What's the point of dancing if you're not having a good time?"

He holds up his hand to silence me. "*However*," he says, "if you're going to dance in a professional ballet, you have to do what the choreographer has planned. Choreographing the dance is her job, not yours. Do you understand?"

"Sure," I say. I don't want to choreograph the whole dance. But once I get the steps down, I'm sure the choreographer won't mind if I spice things up a little. I'm sure she'll want the dance to be as good as it can be—and that might mean throwing in a few Epatha touches.

"Good," he says, standing up. "Congratulations again. I'm sure your family will be very proud of you."

The proud-family thing? Mr. Lester got that right.

I make the announcement as soon as I get home. It's a slow time in the restaurant, so I call Abuela and Nonna down from our apartment upstairs. My family hardly ever sits together in a booth—everyone's usually too busy—but this time I make them. Having them fuss over me all at once will be more fun than having them each make little individual fusses.

I stand at the end of the booth and clear my throat. "We had the auditions for *Springtime in Harlem* today," I say, "*and...*"

Mama and Abuela lean forward at the same moment. Nonna scrunches up her face, as if daring anyone not to give her granddaughter a role. Papa sweeps back what little is left of his hair, which he always does when he's nervous.

"Well? Well?" he asks.

"I got the main part!" I say. "Well, the main part for kids."

Nonna jumps up much more quickly than you'd expect someone her size to be able to jump. She squeezes my face in her hands. "Our little star! Our *stella piccola!*" she says, kissing me enthusiastically on both cheeks.

"That's wonderful, darling!" my mother says, standing up to hug me.

"*¡Fabuloso!* You must get your talent from me," Abuela says.

Dad's eyes shine. "Well," he says. "Well. Tonight we celebrate!"

"Tickets!" Mom says. "We need lots of tickets. We'll invite the Mitchells, and the Smiths, and the Browns, and the Harringtons...and of course, your cousin Reece...."

"Mom!" I say. "The show's not for weeks. I'm sure there will be time to get tickets."

"This isn't just a school ballet show, Epatha," Mom says. "This is the big time! The Harlem Ballet!"

That's when it all sinks in. It *is* the big time! I feel like a star, even when Mom sends me upstairs to do my homework. I try to focus on my math problems, but adding fractions is hard when your head's filled with sparkling costumes and spotlights.

That night I dream I'm dancing across the stage of the Harlem Ballet theater in a bright red tutu. My friends are onstage with me, but they're in the background. I do a stunning series of pirouettes, then take a bow. A woman rushes onstage. She's a big Broadway producer. She wants me to drop out of school and star in a show! *I guess this means I don't need to learn how to add fractions after all*, I think as I sign the contract.

CHAPTER
6

"HEY, STAR," AL SAYS ON TUESDAY AS I WALK INTO THE WAIT-ing room and join her, Brenda, and the triplets on our usual bench.

I'm a little embarrassed. But not *too* embarrassed. "Hey," I say.

Terrel comes in and slings her bag under the bench. I wonder if she's mad about not getting the part.

"Hey, Terrel," I say.

"Hi," she says. "Has anyone seen my blue sweater? I think I left it here Saturday."

"Someone would have picked it up by now," says Jessica. "Why don't you ask in the office?"

Terrel comes back with her sweater balled up in her hands. "They had it," she says, sitting down beside me.

She takes off her sneakers and starts pulling on her ballet shoes. "Congratulations on getting the role," she says gruffly.

"Thanks," I say. "I wish we could have both gotten it."

She squints at me and grins. "No, you don't," she says.

I smile. "You're right—I don't. You know I want to be a ballet star. This will be good training."

"It's going to be twice as much work for me," she says.

"What do you mean?"

"I'm your understudy. Remember? That means I have to learn your part *and* my part." She gives an exaggerated sigh. "So I can do the part if you break an ankle or get the plague or something."

"Jerzey Mae, she's kidding. The plague is extremely rare in this country," Brenda says, before Jerzey Mae can freak out.

As Brenda explains to Jerzey Mae exactly *how*

rare the plague is, I turn to Terrel. "You're not mad?" I ask her.

"Nah." She shakes her head. "It would have been fun to get the part, but you won it, fair and square. What did Mr. Lester say to you afterward?"

I bend over to put my shoes under the bench. "Nothing, really. He just wanted to make sure I'd do the right steps instead of making stuff up."

Terrel tilts her head as she considers this. "He's got a point," she says. "You always add your own moves. That can be good, but you can't do that in a big show."

"I *know*, Terrel," I say, a little annoyed. "Mr. Lester already told me, okay?"

"Okay, okay," she says. "I was just trying to help."

I almost say that if she was such an expert, she'd have gotten the part. But I decide that wouldn't be very nice. She's probably a *little* disappointed, even if she's not admitting it.

After Ms. Debbé leads our class, the girls who aren't in the show leave, and Mr. Lester comes in. Ms. Debbé sits down in a chair at the side of the studio, and Mr. Lester takes her place in the front of the room.

"All right, girls," he says. "Since this is a new ballet, I want to tell you a little about it before we get started. That way you'll all know how your parts fit into the story."

A thrill of excitement goes through me. I'd almost forgotten that this is a *new* ballet. No one in the world has ever danced in it before. I jab Jessica with my elbow. She grins.

Mr. Lester continues. "*Springtime in Harlem* is about a young man who moves to Harlem in the

1930s, during the Harlem Renaissance. Do any of you know what that was?"

Jerzey raises her hand eagerly. "Like a Renaissance fair? With princesses and knights?"

JoAnn rolls her eyes. "You think there were knights running up and down 125th Street in the 1930s, you nut?"

"It was a time when there was an explosion of art, music, and dancing in Harlem," Mr. Lester explains. "The ballet tells the story of a young man who moves to Harlem from a small town because he hopes to become a dancer. The music will be wonderful—lots of jazz from that era. And the choreography, by Anita Burton, is inspired by some of the popular dances from back then." He pauses, as if for effect. "And I'm happy to tell you that the part of the young man will be danced by Linc Simmons."

"*The* Linc Simmons?" I ask.

"The famous one?" Al says.

Jerzey Mae chimes in. "The really cute one?"

Mr. Lester nods. "Yes, the famous, really cute one. But I'm counting on you girls not to go crazy around him. You need to act like professionals. Right?"

We all nod.

But still—Linc Simmons! He's amazing. I saw him dance on TV just a few weeks ago, on a PBS special. He did this totally wild new dance where he was jumping and flailing around all over the place. He's exactly the kind of dancer I want to be—full of emotion and expression.

"He won't be rehearsing with you until the week before the show, so keep your autograph books at home till then," Mr. Lester says. "Now—your scene is near the beginning of the ballet. It's a street scene, with lots of dancers onstage. It's the day Linc's character arrives in Harlem, and he's exploring the city for the first time. He's excited by all the movement and people and music." As he talks, Mr. Lester seems to come alive. He starts walking through Linc's role, as though he can't help himself. I sometimes forget that he used to dance with the Harlem Ballet himself.

"He sees a group of girls playing on the street and stops to dance with them," he continues, leaping gracefully over to the side of the room. "All seven of you are dancing together at first." He bows and extends his hand to an imaginary person. "But then he takes one of the girls—that's you, Epatha—by the hand and does a short dance with her on the street before he moves on. Got it?"

He takes her *by the hand*? I get to touch Linc Simmons's hand? And dance with him? I shiver with excitement.

"You're so lucky," says Al. "I might have tried a little harder if I'd known I'd get to dance with Linc Simmons!"

"You'll all get to be plenty close to Linc," Mr. Lester says. "I hope you'll focus as much on learning your parts as you do on Mr. Simmons. We're here to do a dance, ladies, not form a fan club. Right?"

Jerzey Mae's eyes are popping out of her head. Jessica is smiling off into the distance. Even JoAnn and Al look a little star-struck. "Linc Simmons," JoAnn says, under her breath.

Mr. Lester closes his eyes and shakes his head. "All right, even if you *do* form a fan club, you need to know the dance. Let's get started."

CHAPTER

7

SINCE WE ALL DANCE TOGETHER AT FIRST, WE START BY rehearsing together. After we learn the opening section of the dance, we split up. Ms. Debbé takes the other girls into another room to learn their parts.

Mr. Lester and I stay behind so he can teach me my role.

"Pirouettes across the stage—right; then you take Linc's hand." He holds out his hand and I take it. "Spin, spin, spin—that's right."

Pretty soon I have the basics down.

"Good work, Epatha," he says. "So, the key emotion here is joy. You're hanging out with your friends.

It's a beautiful day. You're having a good time danc-ing with them, and then with this new fellow."

Joy. I can definitely do joy, especially if Linc Sim-mons is involved.

After a few more run-throughs, we work on put-ting the dance to the music, which makes it even more fun. As I do a jeté, I wave my arms in what I think is a very joyful fashion.

"Epatha," Mr. Lester says firmly, "that's not in the dance."

"Sorry," I say. *It* should *be*, I think.

Near the end of the session, Terrel comes in.

"We're done," she says to Mr. Lester. "Ms. Debbé told me I should come in so I can learn this part, too."

"Absolutely," he says. "Why don't you watch Epatha go through her dance once; then we'll do it again and you can dance along with her."

I like the part where we're showing Terrel the dance. I especially like dancing with Mr. Lester, because I'm already imagining what it'll be like to dance with Linc.

I am not so crazy about the part where we do the dance again and Terrel's right behind me. I can almost feel her breathing down my neck.

"Very good, Terrel," Mr. Lester says, sounding impressed. "You're picking things up really fast. Let me just show you that middle section again."

I watch as he takes her hand, spins her around, and then shows her the sequence of steps that follows.

"Want to try the whole thing?" he asks. She nods.

Okay, I have to admit it: she's good. She stumbles a little at the start, because she forgets which way to turn, but she learns the dance a lot faster than I did. However, when they run through it a second time, I notice that it looks exactly the same. Exactly! When she does the big jump at the end, she even lands on the exact same spot on the floor. What kind of dancing is that?

"Terrific," Mr. Lester says. "You both did a great job today. But keep practicing at home, please. You need to have the dance down cold. That way your bodies will do what they're supposed to do even if you get nervous. Or," he adds, "a little starstruck by a certain Mr. Simmons."

Terrel and I walk downstairs together. "How was the other rehearsal?" I ask her.

"Good," she says. "Everyone learned the dance quickly."

We walk in silence for minute. Then I say, "Linc Simmons!"

She grins. "I know. Crazy, huh? And you get to hold his hand."

"You'll probably get to practice with him, too," I say.

Terrel stops, right in the middle of the stairs. "Really?"

I nod.

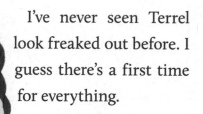

I've never seen Terrel look freaked out before. I guess there's a first time for everything.

JOY, JOY, JOY. MR. LESTER SAID THE DANCE SHOULD BE FULL of joy. That's not going to be too hard for me! I fly up the stairs at home and nearly knock Nonna over.

"How was your first rehearsal, *stella piccola*?" asks Nonna.

"Good!" I say. "And I get to dance with Linc Simmons!"

Nonna's furrows her brow. "How are you going to dance with persimmons? They are a fruit, no?"

Nonna is a little hard of hearing sometimes. "Not persimmons, Nonna. Linc Simmons. The famous dancer. Remember? The one we saw on TV?"

She nods, but I can tell she has no idea who I'm talking about.

Abuela, however, is a different story. "Linc Simmons? You're dancing with *the* Linc Simmons?"

I nod. I'm smiling so big that my cheeks hurt.

Abuela just stands there. I don't think I've ever seen her at a loss for words before. Finally, she rushes forward and gives me an enormous hug. "Well, of *course* you're dancing with Linc Simmons! You're my granddaughter!"

Nonna comes over to hug me, too. Even if she doesn't know who Linc is, she's not going to let Abuela make a bigger fuss. "Simmons! Simmons!" she says.

Sandwiched between them, I can barely breathe. I wriggle away just as Mom comes upstairs.

"Simmons!" Nonna calls triumphantly, motioning to me. "She is dancing with Simmons!"

"What?" Mom asks, clearly confused.

Abuela cuts in. "*My* granddaughter is dancing with Linc Simmons in that big fancy Harlem Ballet show!"

"That dancer we just saw on TV?" Mom asks. "The cute one?"

"Ewww, Mom!" I say. Linc may be cute, but I don't want to hear my mom saying it.

"Yes, the cute one!" Abuela says.

Or my grandma.

"I get to do a solo dance with him at the beginning of the show," I say, hoping to distract them from the "cute" thing.

"I need to go sell some more tickets!" Abuela says.

"I also need to," says Nonna. They race for the phone. Nonna, surprisingly, overtakes Abuela, and we hear a triumphant "Ha!" as she gets there first.

At least Mom isn't going completely crazy. But then she says, "Maybe I'll go e-mail a few friends about this. Can't let your grandmas sell more tickets than I do!" She kisses my head and dashes off.

Linc Simmons fever has officially struck, and I'll bet even Brenda doesn't have a cure for it.

51

CHAPTER
9

WE STAY AFTER CLASS EVERY TUESDAY AND SATURDAY TO work on our dances, and they're looking good. I do the steps I'm supposed to do, even though it's hard to resist adding a flourish here and there. But I understand that I need to know the steps so well I could do them in my sleep. *Then* I can add the finishing touches.

Everyone's a little jumpy, especially with the Linc factor and all. After class one day, as we're changing shoes, Jerzey Mae says, "I wish we could practice more than twice a week."

"You do, you goofball," JoAnn says. "You and Jessica are always in one of your rooms practicing."

"That's not *all* of us," says Jerzey Mae. "It's different when we're together."

"Hey, I know," I say. "You guys could all come over and practice in the restaurant supply room. Like we did last year, when we had to teach Al how to spin. *¡Problema resuelto!* Problem solved."

"I don't know," says Terrel. "Last year it was just Al dancing. We need space for all six of us to dance at the same time."

"We can move some of the boxes around to make room," I say. "And I can help you guys. I can watch and see if you're doing anything wrong."

Terrel and JoAnn exchange a look.

"Let's do it!" Jessica says. "I want to practice all we can, so we're perfect by opening night."

💕

So the next day, all my friends come to Bella Italia after school and we head for the back.

JoAnn even brings a little speaker for her tablet,

so that they can dance to the music. We push back the pasta boxes and large cans of tomatoes to clear some floor space.

They take their places. "Aren't you dancing with us?" Jerzey Mae asks. "At least for the first section?"

"Nah," I say. "I've got my part down."

I sit on a big container of olive oil and take charge of the tablet controls. "Okay, you guys—get ready," I say.

As the music starts, they begin their dance. I watch as they spin and jump. They look pretty good,

but they seem kind of stiff, to me. As they dance, I give them some helpful comments. "You could jump a little higher, Terrel," I say. "Brenda, put some feeling into it, girl! You guys are supposed to be having fun! JoAnn, why don't you try an extra little spin there?"

JoAnn comes over, takes the tablet, and stops the music. She looks mad, for some reason. "Excuse me. Did someone make you the director of this show?"

"No...What are you talking about?" I ask.

Jessica hurries over. "I think JoAnn just means it's a little hard for us to dance with you making comments all the time," she says gently.

"What? That's nuts!" I say. "Mr. Lester and Ms. Debbé talk all the time while we're dancing."

"Yeah, and *they* actually know what they're talking *about*. Because they're our *teachers*," Terrel replies.

My scalp tingles the way it does when I'm furious. Jerzey Mae's eyes are wide, as if she's waiting for an explosion. Jessica, who hates any kind of fighting, looks totally freaked out. There's a moment of complete silence that seems to last for hours.

"Fine," I finally say. "I was just trying to help."

Everyone relaxes a little. "Shall we start again?" Jessica asks quickly. JoAnn reluctantly gives me the tablet back. I start the music again and sit and watch them. Very quietly. I don't say a single word. Since I'm the one with the starring role, it seems like they might actually *want* my help, but they can suit themselves.

The music ends. "That felt pretty good," Brenda says.

"Except the very last part," Al says. "We were a little too slow on those spins."

I nod vigorously. They were *way* too slow on the spins. Jerzey Mae looks at me, then looks away quickly.

"Thanks for letting us practice here, Epatha," Jessica says. "That was really helpful."

"Yeah, thanks," Al says stiffly.

"You're welcome," I say. I'd been planning to show them *my* dance, but I decide not to. I don't think they deserve to see it. "You want to hang around in the restaurant?"

They look at one another. "No, thanks," JoAnn says. "We should be getting home."

"Me, too," says Terrel. "I have lots of homework."

They file out of the storage room into the restaurant. Even though it's still early, there are a bunch of customers already. Dad is putting plates heaped with pasta in front of a few gray-haired ladies.

"Hello, girls," he says. "How are my favorite ballerinas? Did you have a good rehearsal?"

"Yes, thanks," says Jessica.

They weave past the tables toward the door. Mom, who is refilling all the salt shakers, says, "No breadsticks today, girls? You're welcome to stay for dinner if you'd like."

"We have to go," Terrel says.

"Bye, guys," I say as the glass door swings shut behind them.

Mom looks puzzled. She comes over and puts her hand on my shoulder. "Is something wrong, *cariño*?"

I shake my head. "Nope. Some people just don't want helpful feedback."

"Were you being critical of their dancing?" she asks. "I can see how they might not appreciate that."

"I was trying to help them!" I said. "I didn't say all bad things. I said some good ones too. I think." I try to remember if I actually did.

I don't like the way Mom's looking at me. "What? I've heard *you* telling *your* friends what's wrong with them," I say. "Like in your writers' group."

Mom's writing group meets in the restaurant every week. They're always talking about one another's work and picking it apart.

"*Querida*, that's different. We're all in that group because we want to help each other improve our writing. And we *ask* each other for suggestions. Did your friends ask you for your input?"

"Not exactly," I admit.

She raises her eyebrows.

"Okay," I finally say. "But I *was* trying to help."

Mom pours salt into the last shaker, then starts screwing the lids back on. "If Terrel had gotten the role, do you think you'd appreciate her giving you suggestions?"

But she didn't get it! I think. Mom is missing the point. But I know what she wants me to say. "No."

She nods. "Okay." She kisses the top of my head and gives me a gentle push toward the door to our apartment. "Homework time," she says.

But instead of doing my homework, I practice my dance. When I do, I feel the music pouring through my body—even when there's no music playing. Sometimes it comes out in a flick of my foot, or an extra kick, or a twirl of my head.

Every time I practice, I throw in something new. I do the choreographer's steps, like Mr. Lester said, but I improve on them a little. How could anyone object to that? She'll probably be happy that I'm making her dance better. Doing things the same way over and over is boring. You have to spice it up!

"Is that the dance you are doing with the Linc boy?" Nonna asks, poking her head in my doorway.

"Yep," I say.

Abuela joins her. "Let's see it, *cariño*! Can we have a preview?"

I smile. "Sure." I perform it for them, humming the music as I do. When I finish, they both applaud really loudly.

"*Favoloso!* You will be wonderful. And already I have five friends coming to see your show."

"And *I* have nine!" Abuela says, winking at me.

Nonna grunts. I'm betting some arms will be twisted down at the Italian American hall next week during her bingo game.

"Our granddaughter—the star of the show!" Abuela says.

"This, at least, we agree on," sniffs Nonna.

"Abuela, I'm not *exactly* the star," I say. But I flush with pleasure.

"Hmph!" Nonna says. "You are the star girl. You are dancing with the Simmons Linc boy. I think that means you are the star."

Maybe she's right!

By the time I get around to my homework, all that dancing and star talk has put me back in a really good mood. As I lie in bed that night, I see myself onstage again, but this time taking a bow with Linc. We both get huge bouquets. He pulls a rose from his and hands it to me.

I fall asleep with a smile on my face.

CHAPTER
10

WE CONTINUE TO WORK ON OUR DANCES. MS. DEBBÉ AND Mr. Lester are both happy with how they're coming along.

When I practice mine, Terrel is there most of the time, dancing along with me. Mr. Lester has her do it alone sometimes, too, just to make sure she knows the steps. She still looks like a little mechanical doll when she's dancing: every step perfectly in place. But after the storeroom incident, I keep my observations to myself.

One day, we head over to the triplets' house, because Jerzey Mae says she has a surprise for us.

"What? Did you decide to organize your pencils by length instead of by color?" asks JoAnn.

"Shut up, JoAnn," says Al, but she's smiling. Jerzey Mae's a little crazy where neatness and organization are concerned.

"No," Jerzey Mae says, pained. "You'll see."

When we get there, we go into her very tidy room and sit on the floor. She pulls her computer over and pulls up YouTube.

"It's Linc!" Jessica says. We all lean forward to see better. "How did you find that, Jerz?"

"My friend Paula told me about it," Jerzey Mae says, pleased with herself. "Her dad works in TV. This is a dance special that was on TV in Germany, but hasn't been on TV here yet. Paula said Linc has a big solo dance in it—just a sec." She fast-forwards, finds the right place on the video, and presses the play button.

There's Linc, alone on the stage. He's wearing a tank top and tights, with a gold crown on his head and gold bands around his arms. The tank top has strips of fabric that flutter around as he moves, almost like wings. He faces one way, then another. He turns and spins and jumps around like some sort of maniac. Every once in a while, there's a close-up of his face; he even looks crazy. We all watch, enthralled, as he leaps and twirls across the screen.

"What the heck's he doing?" JoAnn asks. "Looks like he's got ants in his pants."

"He looks like a wild animal trapped in a cage," Jessica says.

Jerzey Mae shakes her head. "Nope. He's a prince," she says. "This is the scene where he goes crazy because he's lost his true love."

There's so much power in every one of his moves. You can *feel* the emotion as he dances. Jessica's right: he does seem like he's trapped and desperate. And I *know* he has to be adding in his own little touches. How could a choreographer plan out all those twists and turns?

After the dance is over, Jerzey Mae closes out of the video.

"Whew," Al says. "Pretty intense."

"Now, *that*," I say, "is dancing."

My friends nod their heads in agreement.

A smile creeps across Brenda's face. "We're going to be onstage with him in two weeks!"

"Even less than that," Terrel says. "The *show* is in two weeks. He'll have to be at some rehearsals. Maybe the one next Wednesday." Wednesday is our first practice at the theater—the actual Harlem Ballet theater. My stomach tightens up just a little at the thought.

JoAnn snorts. "A big star like him? He probably just swoops in the night of the show."

"No way," Terrel says. "Big stars rehearse, too."

"Not as much as everyone else," Al replies.

"Mr. Lester says the Harlem Ballet has been practicing for weeks."

"Yeah, but this is special," Brenda says. "I overheard Mr. Lester saying that the choreographer designed this ballet specially, so Linc didn't have to rehearse with the company very much."

"Why?" Jessica asks.

"Because he's Linc! And the choreographer really wanted him in the show, but Linc's schedule was really full. So, in this ballet, a lot of the time, he's dancing alone. The choreographer flew to Germany, where Linc was last performing, to teach him his role."

Terrel continues, "Well, *anyway*, he has to practice his dance with Epatha. And maybe with me."

I'm sure she hopes she'll get to practice with him. I don't know why she needs to, though. I don't plan to get sick, or trip on a skateboard, like JoAnn did.

Brenda interrupts my thoughts. "I should go," she says. "Homework."

"*Real* homework?" Terrel asks. "Or Brenda homework?" Since Brenda wants to be a doctor, she's decided that this spring she will memorize every single bone and muscle in the human body. And believe me, there are a lot of them.

"Doesn't matter," Brenda says, standing up.

"Brenda homework." JoAnn grins.

As I practice my dance that night, I imagine I'm as wild as Linc was in the video. I make my arms flail around. I spin. I try to stare as intensely as he did. As I turn the dance's boring old single turn into an

Epatha special triple turn, I notice Nonna watching me with a look of concern on her face.

"Are you angry?" she asks. "What is wrong with my little *tesoro*?"

I shake my head. "Just practicing," I say.

"But I thought this dance was about a happy little girl. You look like an unhappy eagle."

I'm not sure where the eagle thing came from. But I guess she's right that the dance needs to look happy.

"I'm still working on it," I say.

She shakes her head and moves on. I try being wildly happy instead of just plain wild. Finally, I think I've got it: the perfect combination of happiness and creative steps. And next week, I'll be showing Mr. Linc Simmons exactly how good a dancer I am.

CHAPTER
11

WOW. WOW, WOW, WOW.

We're standing in front of the Harlem Ballet theater. It's Wednesday afternoon, and we're about to go inside for our first rehearsal here. We even got to leave school early. When I gave my teacher, Mrs. Philips, the note from my dad, she was very impressed. "You're dancing at the Harlem Ballet? That's really something!" she said. She was not impressed, however, enough to let me off the hook for tomorrow's math homework.

"Look!" I shout. "There's a poster!"

Linc's picture smiles out at us from a poster hung in front of the theater. We cluster around. "*Two Weeks Only*: Springtime in Harlem," I read aloud. "*Starring Linc Simmons.*"

"And us!" Brenda says, pointing to some much smaller print at the bottom.

I squint. "*And featuring students from the Nut-cracker School of Ballet.*"

"Wow!" Jerzey Mae says. "We're famous!"

"Hmph," I say. "They could have made us a little more famous by not using teeny-weeny letters." *And by putting my name on there, too*, I think. After all, I *am* the one dancing with Linc.

"Girls!" Ms. Debbé says. "Time to go in."

She pushes the front door open, and we walk into the theater lobby. A red plush carpet stretches from one gold wall to the other. A huge chandelier hangs from the ceiling; it's so big that I scoot out from under it, because it looks as if it might crash to the ground at any moment. A bar wraps around the left side, and a big, elegant stairway swoops up along the right wall to the balcony.

It takes a lot to shut us all up, but the sight of the lobby does it. Even JoAnn's eyes are popping out of her head, and she's never excited about *anything*.

Ms. Debbé smiles. "Thrilling, is it not? Your first experience dancing in a professional theater. I remember mine well." She closes her eyes and sighs happily.

One of the doors leading into the theater swings. open. "Hello, girls," Mr. Lester says. He seems distracted. "Why don't you go on—Hey!" A big smile breaks out on his face. "There you are!"

He walks past us, his hand extended. We turn around to see Linc Simmons, standing there in all his glory. A tiny squeak escapes Jerzey Mae's throat.

"Hi there," Linc says, smiling and stepping forward to shake Mr. Lester's hand. He's not as tall as I thought he'd be, and it's weird seeing him in jeans and a jacket when we're used to seeing him in all sorts of exotic costumes. But he's still very, very cute. "I just got into town," Linc continues. "I thought I'd scope out the theater. I've never danced here."

"We know!" Mr. Lester says. "It's time you did. Welcome."

Linc notices us gaping at him. "Hi," he says, smiling. "Who do we have here?"

"These girls will dance in the second scene, the one where you first arrive in Harlem. Say hello, girls."

We murmur hello.

"And this"—Mr. Lester comes over and puts his hand on my shoulder—"is Epatha, the girl you'll be dancing with."

Linc nods. "Hey, Epatha," he says. "I'm looking forward to our duet."

For once I have nothing to say, but I manage a nod.

"Okay." Mr. Lester claps. "Girls, you go on in. Linc, let me take you to the costume designer, so she can do a quick fitting. Then you'll probably want to get some sleep, since we'll be rehearsing pretty much nonstop for the next several days." He turns to us. "Linc's been in Germany for the last month."

Linc nods. "I'm a little tired, that's for sure. Nice meeting you girls," he says, following Mr. Lester into the theater.

We enter the theater, too, just in time to see Linc and Mr. Lester disappear behind the curtain. I'm disappointed that Linc's gone already.

"When do we practice with Mr. Simmons?" Jessica asks Ms. Debbé.

"Tomorrow night," says Ms. Debbé. "Today, the director will work with you girls by yourselves first. But you'll have the chance to dance with the other adults in the scene. Then there will be dress rehearsals Thursday and Friday nights."

The theater is mostly dark, as if there was going to be a performance. But the stage is all lit up. There are three dancers rehearsing onstage. The two guys are wearing T-shirts and tights, and the woman is wearing a faded blue unitard with leg warmers and a scarf.

A man and two women sit in the audience several rows back from the front. As we get closer, I see that the man is Mr. Tonetti. He talks to one of the women while she scribbles things down on a notepad. He moves his arms and hands around wildly while he talks, which makes him look like he's mad, but I can't see his face to know for sure.

Mr. Lester slips back into the theater and joins us. He waits until Mr. Tonetti is done waving his arms around. "Mr. Tonetti?" he says, hesitantly. This is weird. Mr. Lester always seems very cool and in control of things, but it looks like he's a little afraid of Mr. Tonetti.

Mr. Tonetti turns around to face us. "Yes?" He blinks, then rivets his gaze on us. "Ah. The girls."

"Yes. This is—" It seems as though Mr. Lester is just about to introduce us when Mr. Tonetti interrupts.

"Good." He claps loudly for attention. The dancers onstage stop dancing and look.

"That is enough for now. We'll move on to scene two," Mr. Tonetti says.

The dancers leave, stopping to scoop up the water bottles and sweaters they've left at the sides of the stage. The clipboard woman scurries up the steps and disappears, maybe to get the other scene-two dancers.

Mr. Tonetti looks at us. "You have practiced?"

What kind of question is that? I wonder. Of course we've practiced.

Mr. Lester jumps in. "They've done a great job. They all know their parts very well."

Mr. Tonetti makes a noise in his throat. "Very well. To the stage, please," he says.

Mr. Lester leads us down the side aisle. It feels like a very long trip. When we get to the front, Mr. Lester tells us we can leave our things in the front-row seats. We're already wearing our dance clothes, but we sit down in the plush velvet seats to put on our ballet slippers.

"Wow," Al says under her breath. The theater air smells of dust and sweat. Jessica pulls down the seat beside mine. It squeaks as she sits in it.

"Can you believe we're here?" she whispers.

I shake my head. Terrel, on my other side, is glaring at a spot on the floor. I recognize this as her concentrating glare, not her mad glare. I bet she's running over our dance in her mind, although she doesn't need to; she's got it down pat.

"Girls: onstage, please," Mr. Lester says.

We stand up and walk to the side of the stage, but Jerzey Mae, who is in front, hesitates at the bottom of the stairs as if she's afraid to go up.

Well, I'm not! I take the lead, and my friends follow behind me.

CHAPTER
12

THE STAGE FEELS EVEN BIGGER THAN IT LOOKS FROM THE audience. Pieces of masking tape mark the black floor. The stage lights, which didn't seem all that bright before, are blinding. As if in response to our squinting, the lights come down. Suddenly we can see all the seats. There are a lot of them.

"This theater must hold hundreds of people," I whisper to Brenda.

"More like one thousand, two hundred," she whispers back. "I counted the rows and the seats in each row and multiplied."

I imagine every seat filled and every person's eyes on us as we do our dance. A thrill goes through my body.

Jerzey Mae, however, is looking a little sick. "More than a thousand?" she says.

Mr. Tonetti motions for Mr. Lester to come over, and they whisper for a moment. Then Mr. Lester comes back and stands in front of the stage. It feels weird that we're taller than he is. He looks up at us.

"Mr. Tonetti would like to see your part of the dance alone, first," he says. "Then we'll bring some of the adult dancers in." He turns around. "With music?" he asks Mr. Tonetti. Mr. Tonetti nods.

Mr. Lester hops onstage and shows us exactly where we'll be standing when the curtain goes up; so that's what those pieces of masking tape on the floor are for. We take our places, and he jumps back down, but not before giving us an encouraging smile.

The music seems to come out of nowhere. In the ballet studio, we have a little stereo system in the corner. Here, the music surrounds us. I feel its joy, its happiness, fill my body.

We all start dancing together. Here on the big stage, I leap higher, twirl faster, than I ever have before. We dance as a unit, leaping left, leaping right, doing a series of turns.

Then it's time for my solo. Since Linc isn't dancing with us yet, I do the dance by myself. I reach out my hand as though he were taking it. I leap left, then do three pirouettes to the right, keeping my gaze on an imaginary spot on the back wall so I don't get dizzy. I'm aware of my friends' continuing on with their part of the dance, but I'm focused on my own part. The music inspires me so much that I do an Epatha special triple spin that takes me to the other side of the stage, and then jeté back over to where I'm supposed to be.

The music stops abruptly. "Epatha!" Terrel hisses. "What are you doing? That's not in the dance!"

I turn to stare at her. "I was inspired," I say.

"You'd better uninspire yourself fast, girlfriend," she says.

This makes me mad. "*Some* of us think dancing with emotion is important," I say.

"I'm trying to help you, you show-off," she whispers heatedly. "You can't just—"

"*What* did you call me?" I ask.

"You gotta do what you're supposed to, E.!"

"Dance like a little robot, you mean?"

Hurt flashes across Terrel's face; then her expression hardens. But I'm all riled up and just keep talking. "I think you're just trying to get the part yourself, that's what I think."

"I can't believe—" Terrel begins.

But Mr. Lester has jumped onstage and is coming over to us, so she can't finish her sentence. He has a very serious look on his face. "Epatha." He takes me to the side of the stage and into the wings. "I thought I'd warned you that you can't just cut loose up here. The woman beside Mr. Tonetti is Ms. Burton, the choreographer. You have to respect her work. You need to do her steps, not your own."

My skin feels hot and prickly. I would have thought Mr. Lester would understand.

"You do know the steps, right?" he asks, as if I'm a three-year-old.

I nod.

"Then do them, please," he says. "We'll take it from the top again."

I look out into the audience, where Mr. Tonetti and Ms. Burton are sitting. I'd been thinking they might actually *like* me to spice up their ballet a little. Look at the way Linc dances! It's pretty clear he's doing his own thing, letting the music move him.

Almost as though I've summoned him, a side door opens, and Linc comes in. My heart is in my throat. He wanders up and sits down a few seats over from Mr. Tonetti. My friends are all totally silent, but I can see from the looks on their faces that they've seen Linc, too. He's going to watch us dance tonight! Right now!

"Places!" Mr. Lester says. We go back to the bits of tape that mark the places where we're supposed to start. The music begins. I'm so excited I can hardly stay still—but I don't have to. We start the dance again. I do what Mr. Lester said and perform exactly the steps I was given.

But then it's time for my solo. I'm hoping that Linc will jump onstage and dance with me, but he doesn't. That's okay—he's watching! I want to dance bigger and better and brighter than I ever have before. I want him to know I'm a kindred spirit, someone who dances just like he does, with passion and excitement. The music sweeps over me and through me. I'm a little aware that I'm not doing exactly what I'm supposed to be doing, but I'm dancing with joy and power, and that's what it's all about.

The music stops again. I turn and look out into the audience.

Mr. Tonetti has motioned Mr. Lester back again. He and Ms. Burton talk to Mr. Lester. Mr. Tonetti's using his hands. A lot. I look over to see if Linc has noticed my fabulousness, but I can't see his face from here.

Mr. Lester jogs to the front of the stage. "Epatha, I need to talk to you," he says quietly. "Girls," he says in a louder voice, "start again, from the beginning. Terrel, you take Epatha's role."

My friends exchange glances, probably not sure what's happening. Terrel steps over to my spot onstage.

"Let's go into the lobby, Epatha," Mr. Lester says. "Bring your things."

My face burns. I can feel my friends looking at me, but I don't want to look at them. I gather my stuff and follow Mr. Lester up the aisle. I pass right by Linc, but I can't look at him, either. Usually, I like being the center of attention, but this definitely does not feel like a good thing. As we continue up the aisle, Mr. Tonetti calls, "Take it from the top," and the music starts.

Mr. Lester holds the swinging door open for me, and then we're in the lobby. I don't think I've ever seen him angry before, but he looks angry now. Even worse, he looks disappointed.

"Epatha, I told you from the beginning you needed to do the steps you were given. Didn't I?" He looks at me, waiting for a response.

"Yes, I guess," I say. "But—"

"No buts," he says. "I really pushed for you when we were casting the solo part. Mr. Tonetti wanted Terrel, but I talked him into giving you a chance."

I stare at the carpet.

His tone grows more gentle. "I'm sorry, Epatha, but we have to pull you from the show."

I have an image of someone coming up and pulling on my arm as I'm onstage. "What do you mean, *pull* me?" I ask.

"What I mean is that Terrel will take your part. I don't have time to teach you the chorus dance, so I'm afraid this means you won't be dancing in the performance."

I can't have heard him right. Me? I'm the best dancer in our class! How can he take me out of the show?

"Give me another chance," I hear myself saying. "I promise, I'll do exactly what I'm supposed to." *Even if it is kind of boring*, I think.

He shakes his head. "I'm sorry. Mr. Tonetti is the director, and I have to say, in this case I think he's right. You're a wonderful dancer, Epatha, but you need to follow the rules."

I'm so sick of hearing about rules. Linc doesn't follow stupid rules, I almost say, but for once I have the sense to keep my mouth shut.

"Will you be okay getting home?" he asks. "Do you want me to call your parents? Or do you want to wait out here until they come to get you at six?"

My parents! It feels as if someone's socked me in the stomach. What are my parents going to say? And Nonna and Abuela? "No," I say quickly. "I live just around the corner. I'll be fine."

"I'm sorry, Epatha," he says again. "I know this is difficult."

I don't respond. I just walk out the door with my head high.

CHAPTER
13

I DON'T LIVE FAR FROM THE THEATER, BUT MY WALK HOME IS the longest walk I've ever taken. In the short time that I was inside, gray clouds have drifted in and covered the city, and a chilly wind has started to blow. A few cold raindrops sting my face, but I brush them away. I've got bigger things to worry about.

At first, I'm just in shock. Not being in the show after all this practicing seems unthinkable, as if it can't possibly be happening.

Then it starts to sink in. And the more it sinks in, the more horrible I feel.

Abuela and Nonna have been competing to see who can sell more tickets to the show. "My granddaughter is dancing with Simmons Linc!" I heard Nonna say on the phone last night. She's never quite gotten Linc's name straight, but what she lacks in accuracy, she makes up for in enthusiasm. She has at least fifteen ladies from the Italian American Social Club coming, and everyone who works at her favorite cannoli shop, to boot.

Not to be outdone, Abuela has been pushing tickets at her gym, at her swing-dancing class, and at the school where she tutors. At breakfast today, she leaned back with a smug smile on her face and told us she'd sold twenty tickets so far. Nonna glared, hmphed loudly, and made a beeline for the phone, undoubtedly to twist the arms of any of her friends who haven't bought tickets yet.

I imagine them all lined up outside the theater, Nonna and Abuela bragging about how their fabulous granddaughter is going to be dancing with Linc Simmons (or Simmons Linc, in Nonna's case). I imagine them filing in and sitting down, talking and laughing with my mom and dad and my friends' parents. I imagine the curtain opening and the dance beginning. And I imagine the looks on their faces when all my friends dance across the stage, but I'm nowhere to be seen.

What am I going to tell them?

The rain is falling harder now, soaking my clothes. The more I think, the madder I get. It isn't fair! This was supposed to be the first big performance in my brilliant dance career. And all I did was dance with passion, just like Linc dances. Why doesn't anyone understand?

I'm soaking wet by the time I get home. A blast of warm air greets me when I push open the restaurant door.

"Epatha! You're drenched, you poor thing!" says Mom.

Nonna stops wiping off a table and scurries over to me. "Soup!" she says. "You need minestrone!"

I shake my head. "No thanks. I'm not hungry."

"We didn't expect you home so soon," Mom says. "Amarah was planning to pick you up at six."

She wraps me in a hug despite the fact that I'm dripping.

"Rehearsal was shorter than I expected," I say. At least that's true. I guess I'll have to tell them what happened eventually, but I'm going to put it off for as long as possible.

"Did you call Amarah?"

I shake my head.

Mom sighs. "I'll do it. You go up and get out of those wet clothes."

I walk toward the door leading to our apartment. My wet shoes squeak against the tiled floor. Normally, I would take advantage of this and dance across the floor to make a symphony of squeaks. Not today.

"Oh, Epatha?" Mom calls after me.

I turn around.

"Amarah's study group is meeting tomorrow night, so I'll take you to rehearsal."

"Great," I say without enthusiasm. I'd thought I could put off telling everyone by having Amarah cover for me—maybe getting her to let me hang out with her for a few hours tomorrow night, when I'd supposedly be rehearsing.

Now I'm really in trouble.

I lie on my bed in my wet clothes. For one minute, I think about going downstairs, gathering everyone together, and just telling them all at once, as if I were pulling off a Band-Aid. It would hurt, but at least I'd get it over with.

But then I think about how disappointed they'd all be. I really hated that disappointed look on Mr. Lester's face. It seems like the only person on earth who might understand me is Linc Simmons. And now that I've been kicked out of his show, I'll never get the chance to talk to him.

There's a knock on my door. I ignore it. When I hear the knob turn, I pretend to be asleep. Through my half-closed eyes, I see Nonna come in, look at me for a moment, then put a bowl of steaming soup on my bedside table before creeping out again.

When she's gone, I sit up and eat the soup. After she finds out that she's sold a billion tickets to see me *not* dance, she'll probably never bring me soup again. I've got to tell them all. But not tonight. Maybe tomorrow.

CHAPTER
14

FOR ONCE I'M ACTUALLY GLAD TO GO TO SCHOOL. LOSING the role sits in my stomach like a rock. Luckily, none of my ballet friends goes to my school. Plus, having to think about math and writing and Greek mythology distracts me a little. Until the final bell rings and I see Mom waiting for me outside the school, smiling. Waiting to walk me to the theater for rehearsal. The rehearsal I don't have anymore.

"Excited?" she asks. "This is your first real dress rehearsal, right?"

I nod and try to look happy.

"So that means you'll be up onstage with all those grown-up dancers, and Linc Simmons and everything?"

I nod.

"Oh!" she says, stopping in the street, "I almost forgot to tell you—a few of your friends called you last night, but it was after you'd fallen asleep. I'm sorry, *querida*. But you'll see them at rehearsal anyway, right?"

I'm glad I was pretending to be asleep. What would I say to them?

We walk up the street. The heavy rain from last night is gone, but it must have sprinkled again recently, because the air smells clean and the sidewalk's a little damp. I walk slowly, because by the time we get to the theater I need to come up with a plan. After Mom drops me off, maybe I can go to the library two blocks away. She'll be really mad if she finds out I went there alone. But the way I figure it, she'll be really mad when I tell her I got kicked out of the show, too, and this will buy me a little time.

"So, do you get to wear costumes today?" Mom asks.

I have no idea. They were going to do the costume

fitting yesterday after the rehearsal, which means that if they did, I missed it. I don't want to lie, so I just say, "Maybe."

Mom turns to me. "Are you okay, Epatha? I thought you'd be a lot more excited." Then a knowing smile spreads across her face. "*Oh.* You're a little nervous, right?"

Well, that's true. "Uh-huh."

She wraps her arm around my shoulders and pulls me close as we walk. "Honey, you are going to be fantastic. You are Epatha the fabulous, right?"

"Yup," I say. "I'm fabulous, all right."

As we approach the theater, I pray I won't run into any of the other kids as they're being dropped off.

Mom checks her cell phone. "We're super-early," she says, wrinkling her nose. "Do you think that's okay?"

"It's fine, Mom," I say, relieved. Being early may at least solve the problem of running into other kids.

We stop in front of the building. "Thanks for dropping me off!" I say brightly. I'm hoping she'll take off so I can scoot to the library without even going into the theater.

No such luck. "I want to peek," she says, her eyes sparkling. "I've walked past this theater a million times, but I've never been inside. I want to see where my little star's going to be dancing."

She pushes open the door for me. What will I do if Mr. Lester's standing in the lobby? *Please, please, please, please, please, be empty*, I think.

It's not empty, but the only person there is some guy restocking the bar. He looks up, then goes back to putting packets of peanuts on the counter. *Phew.*

Mom follows me in. "Oh, my goodness, it's beautiful!" she says, turning to admire the entire lobby. "When was this theater built, do you think?" she asks.

I hop up and down on one foot. I've got to get her out of here before someone sees me. "Mom, I should go"—*Go what?* We're forty-five minutes early!—"warm up. A lot," I say.

She ruffles my hair. "Of course, sweetie. Go get ready." She kisses the top of my head. "Can't wait to see your show!" she calls over her shoulder as she leaves.

I breathe a sigh of relief—until I hear Mr. Lester's voice. He must be inside the theater, and it sounds like he's heading toward the lobby.

I evaluate my options in an instant. If I bolt for the entrance, Mom will see me. So I race to a side door. The curtains separating the theater from the lobby move—Mr. Lester's definitely coming. I push open the door and scramble through it just in time.

I find myself in a hallway that leads to what must be the back of the theater. Fluorescent tubes buzz and cast a harsh light on everything. At the end of the hall, metal stairs stretch down. Mr. Lester had mentioned that there were rehearsal studios underneath the stage.

I tiptoe downstairs, trying to make as little noise as possible. Maybe I can find a room where I can hang out for the whole rehearsal. People aren't going to be practicing downstairs while the actual dress rehearsal is going on, right?

At the bottom of the stairs, another hallway extends to the right. There are metal doors on each side. I listen at the first door and don't hear anything. The door handle moves smoothly when I push it.

Sure enough, it's a rehearsal studio. There's a piano at the side of the room and a wall of mirrors along the back. I could hang out here for a few hours, I think. But now I'm curious about what else is down here.

I go back out to the hallway and stop in front of the next door. I push the handle—and come face to face with Linc Simmons.

CHAPTER
15

"HI, THERE," LINC SAYS, SURPRISED—BUT NOT AS SURPRISED as I am. He's wearing a T-shirt and tights and has a towel around his neck. "I thought I heard someone out in the hall."

This room is another big rehearsal studio that looks almost identical to the first one. A large man with a bushy mustache stands on a ladder in the corner. He and Linc are the only two people in the room.

"Are you lost?" Linc asks. "It's kind of a labyrinth down here." He looks at me more closely. "Hey," he says. "Aren't you the girl I was going to dance with in the second scene?"

My cheeks get hot. He seems to remember what happened—he was watching in the theater yesterday, after all—and starts to say something, then stops. He holds the door open.

"Why don't you come in?" he says. "I was just warming up."

I'm still in shock, but a little spark flares in my brain. I realize that this is it. Somehow, I've been handed a chance to talk to the one person who will understand me. And I'm going to take advantage of it.

"I want to dance like you," I blurt out. "I want to dance the way *I* want to dance. How do I do it? How did *you* do it? I want to dance with passion and emotion and not have to pay attention to stupid rules and choreographers."

"Whoa! Hold on there," Linc says. "Have a seat—uh—what was your name?"

"Epatha." Just saying all that makes me feel a little relieved. All that frustration had been building up inside me for a long time. I hadn't realized how much I'd needed to talk to someone about it. But of course, I couldn't—who would I have talked to? I couldn't even tell my friends how I was feeling.

Linc unfolds a couple of metal chairs and sits down. I sit, too.

"Now, what's this stuff about not having to pay attention to rules?" he asks.

I explain about watching his video. He smiles when I tell him how much we all liked it.

"Your dancing is so wild!" I say. "It was like you were a crazy man. I could tell it was coming from deep down inside you, not from some steps a choreographer made up."

He seems to think for a moment. "You mean this scene?" he asks. He stands up, goes to the center of the studio, and starts doing the crazy-man dance. Goosebumps erupt on my arms. I can't believe I'm sitting five feet away from Linc Simmons and he's dancing for me. Even without music, the dance is every bit as powerful as it was on the TV show—maybe more so, because I see the sweat forming on his brow, and feel the floor thud as he lands each jump.

After a minute, he stops. I applaud. "That was amazing," I say.

"Want to see it once more?" he asks. I nod. He starts the dance again. It's amazing, again.

When he stops, he asks, "Did that look any different from the first time?"

I think about this. Both times looked identical to what I saw on the video.

"I'll do it again," he says. "But first, look at the spot on the floor where I end the dance."

I look. There's a bit of chipped tile there, so it'll be easy to find.

He does the dance again. It looks exactly the same. He ends up in precisely the same place.

A weird feeling starts in my stomach and works its way up to my throat.

"Exactly the same," I say quietly.

He nods. "Does the fact that I did the same choreography make the dance any less powerful or special? Or less passionate?"

I shake my head slowly.

He sits down again. "Epatha, improvising and doing what you want is fine in some situations. But not all the time."

"But why not?" I ask. I still can hardly wrap my head around the idea that he's not just making up his dances as he goes along.

He motions to the lightbulb-changing guy, who was fiddling with a switch on the wall while Linc was dancing. "This is Mac. He's doing me a favor by fixing the lights here, since it's my rehearsal studio. But actually he runs lights for the show." He turns around. "Hey, Mac. If, during my big solo, I ended up at stage right instead of stage left, would that be okay?"

Mac snorts. "We set the lights before the show and program them into the lighting board. If you don't end up where you're supposed to, there won't be a light shining on you. The audience might not even see you."

I hadn't thought of that.

Linc nods. "And if you're dancing with other people, they have to know where you'll be at all times. Otherwise, they might crash into you. That would be dramatic, but not the kind of dramatic you want."

He stops for a moment. "But there's an even more important reason you need to stick to the choreography. A choreographer is an artist, just as much as we dancers are artists. You need to honor the choreographer's work."

"But...but..." I'm at a loss for words. Could I have been so wrong about everything? I've gotten myself kicked out of the show, *and* I said some mean things to Terrel. I feel sick.

She was right. I should have listened to her. No wonder she's the one dancing with Linc.

Linc looks at me. His eyes are soft. "You remind me of me when I was younger, Epatha. I was like you—headstrong and passionate. And want to know a secret?"

I nod.

He leans his head closer. "I ended up losing a part I really wanted, too. For exactly the same reason. I thought I was too talented to have to pay attention to the director. Losing the role hurt, but it was a good lesson. And as soon as I learned it, my career started taking off."

This makes me feel better. But not much. I've wrecked everything. "I told my whole family I was going to dance with you," I say miserably.

Linc seems to consider something. "You really get what I was saying, don't you? About why you need to respect the choreography?"

"Yeah," I say. "I get it. But now it's too late."

"Your friend is doing a good job with the part. But they didn't fill her spot in the dancing chorus. Would you want to take her place there?"

I shake my head. "That Mr. Tonetti guy would never let me do it. And Mr. Lester said he doesn't have time to teach me the part," I say.

"Hmmm," Linc says. "I see your problem. Well, I'm sorry, Epatha. I hope you'll at least come to the show."

I try to imagine what that would feel like. Walking into the big, beautiful theater. Seeing all my friends onstage in their costumes and makeup.

Watching them dance on the same stage as Linc. Hearing the audience cheer for them, while I sit in the audience.

Nope. Not gonna happen.

"You know there's going to be a big party after the first performance, right?" Linc asks.

I nod.

"If you go, come find me and say hi," he says.

Fat chance, I think, but it's still pretty nice of him.

"Now," he continues, "I have to get upstairs for rehearsal." He frowns. "Hey—if you're not in the show, what are you doing here today?"

I don't say anything.

Understanding flashes across his face. "You didn't tell your parents yet, huh?"

I'm glad Linc's such a great guy, and such a good dancer. But does he have to be a mind reader, too?

I shake my head.

"Epatha," he says, suddenly looking more like a grown-up than he did before. "You need to tell them. They're going to find out anyway, right?"

Well, I was hoping they wouldn't. I was starting to make up a brilliant plan, where I'd tell them that I had some horrible disease. Brenda could help me think up something awful to have, I'm sure. But I guess that would mean they'd haul me to the doctor and worry and stuff.

"You can hang out here during today's rehearsal," he says, "but only if you promise me you'll tell them as soon as you go home."

Our eyes lock for a few seconds. Then I look down. "I promise."

"Good," he says. He picks up his water bottle and his bag. And then he holds out his hand. "Bye, Epatha," he says.

I shake his hand. It's not as great as dancing onstage with him. But it's not too bad, either.

CHAPTER
16

MOM IS ALMOST ALWAYS REALLY EARLY TO PICK ME UP. I count on this today, to postpone my fate just a little longer. I keep an eye on the studio clock, and when it's 4:45, I sneak back down the bright hallways, up the stairs, and into the empty lobby. Music drifts out from the theater; rehearsal's still going on, thank goodness. I race through the lobby and out the front door. And there's Mom, checking messages on her phone. There are a few other people hanging around, too, but luckily no one I know.

"Finished already?" Mom asks. "You must have been great if you got to leave early!"

I avoid her questions on the walk home.

But just as we get to Bella Italia, I stop and look right at her. "I have something I need to tell you," I say. My right leg starts shaking. I ignore it and go on. "I need to talk to you and Papa and Nonna and Abuela."

"Is everything okay, sweetie?" she asks.

"I just need to talk to everyone," I say.

As soon as we get home, I march upstairs to the living room. Mom comes in with Dad, who is still in his chef's apron. Then she gets Nonna and Abuela, who are in the kitchen of our apartment, arguing as usual.

Nonna comes in, wiping her hands on a dish towel. Abuela follows. They all sit down.

"What is this about, *piccolina?*" Dad asks.

I take a deep breath. "I'm not going to be dancing in the show," I say.

Nonna gasps and leaps to her feet. "Whose fault is this?" she asks, her voice jumping up three octaves. "I will go talk with them. *Io...io gli do un pugno in faccia!* I will...I will punch them right in the nose!"

The thought of Nonna punching anyone right in the nose would normally be funny, but I don't feel like laughing at the moment.

I motion for her to sit back down. "It's my fault, Nonna," I say. "*Colpa mia.* I made a mistake. I thought I didn't have to do the choreography—the steps—they gave me. So I got kicked out."

There's silence for a moment. "Well," Dad says gruffly. "I'm sure your steps were better than theirs, anyway."

I shake my head. "No, Dad, they weren't. I should've listened to Mr. Lester. And Terrel."

Nonna still looks angry. Abuela just looks sad.

I continue, "Nonna and Abuela, I'm very sorry about you selling all those tickets to the show." I've been doing a good job being strong till now, but here my voice cracks. I am not a crier, but for a horrible moment, I think I'm going to break down in tears. I blink hard.

"Don't worry, *querida*," Abuela says quickly. "*No hay problema.* Not a problem at all."

"Of course not," Nonna says. "My friends, they are all wanting to see this Simmons Linc anyway."

I half smile. "I'm really sorry," I say again quietly. Before, I wondered if I'd get into trouble. But I think they can all see that I'm already so miserable that they can't do anything worse to me than I've already done to myself. "I'm going to go lie down. I'm a little tired," I say. I walk into my room and close my door. Only then do I let the tears come.

CHAPTER
17

I NEVER KNEW WHAT PEOPLE MEANT WHEN THEY SAID, "HAVE a good cry." That's because I didn't get how a cry could be good—until now. After I cry for a while and sniff and blow my nose, I actually do feel better. It still stinks that I won't be in the show. But in a strange way, I feel stronger and more determined. I'm not ever going to let that happen to me again. The next time I'm in a show, I'll do what the director says.

And there's something I have to do: I need to tell Terrel that I'm sorry.

It's almost eight at night. I wonder if it's too late

to call her. Should I apologize in person? I don't do a lot of apologizing, so I don't really know the drill.

Just as I decide it's better to do it now on the phone rather than wait till tomorrow, there's a knock on my door.

"Epatha," Nonna calls, "someone to see you."

That's crazy. Who'd come see me this late? I open my door and peer out.

"Downstairs," Nonna says, motioning in that direction.

"Who is it?" I ask, but she's already waddled back to the kitchen.

I stop in the bathroom to splash a little cool water on my face, then go downstairs and push open the swinging door.

Terrel and all the other Sugar Plums are standing there.

Well, I'd wanted to apologize to Terrel. I hadn't meant to do it in front of everyone. But here goes.

"Terrel," I say, "I'm really, really sorry that I said those things about your dancing. You're a great dancer. Better than me."

She looks a little embarrassed. "Not better," she says. "Different."

"I've been a jerk," I say, looking at all of them. "I'm sorry." My eyes meet Jessica's. Her eyes are so kind that I look away fast so I won't start bawling again.

"Get your dance stuff," Terrel says.

That's the last thing I would have expected her to say. "What? Why?" I ask.

She exhales impatiently. "Because if you're going to learn my chorus role, you need to get your butt in gear. We can only stay till nine o'clock."

"But...but..." I still don't understand, but a flicker of hope dances inside me.

"Linc talked to Mr. Tonetti and Mr. Lester," Terrel says.

"And he talked to us, too," Jessica says.

Al continues, "He asked if we could teach you the part in time for tomorrow's dress rehearsal."

"And since we're the fabulous Sugar Plum Sisters, we said yes," says Brenda, grinning.

"Yeah. If we can teach Al to spin, we can do anything," says JoAnn. Al shoves her.

"Your mom said we can use the back room," Jerzey Mae says.

I stare at them all. I can't believe it.

"Well? Get moving!" orders Terrel.

Learning the dance isn't all that hard. I know the beginning already, of course, and I'd seen them practicing the rest of it. And many of the moves are the same as the ones in the solo dance; it's just the timing that's different.

I do exactly what I'm supposed to do—not one single added arm move or extra jump. And as we're practicing, something strange happens. I realize it actually feels *good* to be moving in unison with my friends.

And I realize something else: I understand that watching six people moving together perfectly might be better than watching five people move perfectly and one do everything a little different. When you watch the Rockettes dance in their Christmas show at Radio City Music Hall, it's not boring because they're all doing the same thing. It's really great because they're all doing *exactly* the same thing.

I think about last fall, when Al first moved to town and we helped her learn to spin in this very room. A lot's happened since then, but here we all are again. Even though I've been a jerk, my friends are all pitching in to help me. I grin so wide I think my face is going to crack. I am one very lucky Sugar Plum.

By nine o'clock, I have it. I really do—every step, every move, every turn. "I'll keep practicing," I tell them as we walk through the restaurant toward the front door.

"You'd better," Terrel says. "Dress rehearsal tomorrow at six p.m. sharp. And you gotta go early, to get fitted for your costume."

"You guys..." I say. They turn around.

I don't have exactly the right words for everything I'm feeling. So I just say, "Thank you. Especially you, Terrel."

I can't help myself. I reach out and give her a big hug.

"Oh, man! Okay, okay," she says, twisting away. Terrel is not a huggy person, but she smiles a little anyway. "See you tomorrow," she says.

CHAPTER
18

I PRACTICE THE DANCE OVER AND OVER ON MY OWN AFTER my friends leave. The next day, I go through it in my head during class, when I'm supposed to be drawing a map of South America. I dance it during gym, while I'm waiting for my turn at bat. And I practice it again after school, in the middle of our living room.

My grandmas are a little confused. They'd just gotten used to the idea of my not being in the show when they found out I was going to be in it after all. "You dance with Simmons Linc again now?" Nonna asks.

"Nope," I said. "Not dancing with Simmons Linc. But dancing in the show. With my friends."

This seems to satisfy her. "Is a good thing I sold thirty-five tickets, then. Which is more than *some* people sold." She looks at Abuela, lifts an eyebrow, and saunters out of the room.

Abuela leans over to me and whispers, "I sold thirty-seven. But I won't tell her right now and ruin her evening." She winks.

Before I know it, it's time for our dress rehearsal. Mom and I walk up the block together. "You're quiet today," she says.

I *am* quiet. I can't wait to perform. But in order to do that, I'm going to have to walk into the theater and face Mr. Lester and Mr. Tonetti. I haven't seen either of them since they kicked me out of the show. I wish my life were a movie and we could just fast-forward to the part where I'm dancing with my friends up on the stage.

As we walk, I'm overcome with a sick, scared feeling. What if it's all a mistake? What if my friends got it wrong? What if Mr. Lester and Mr. Tonetti *didn't* really let me back in the show? What if I walk through the door and they kick me out again? It was humiliating enough the first time. If it happens again, I'm going to have to leave the country.

Mom and I stop in front of the theater door. "You okay?" she asks.

I nod, even though I'm not.

"Want me to come in with you?"

"Nope." Another lie. But if it *is* all a mistake, I don't want my mom to see me get thrown out again.

I scan the street in front of the theater, hoping I'll see one of my friends so I won't have to walk into the theater alone.

The street is totally, completely empty. How can a street in the middle of a big city be so empty?

"See you after rehearsal," I tell Mom, in a fake-cheery voice. I summon my courage and push open the heavy door.

Jessica is standing right there, smiling at me. "There you are," she says, taking my arm. "I was waiting for you."

She *knew*. Relief floods my body. Tears sting my eyes, but they're good tears. I blink them back. With all the crying I've been doing lately, I might as well be Jerzey Mae.

"We need to go right upstairs to the costume room to get you fixed up," Jessica says, pulling me along behind her. "The costume lady was going to try to make Terrel's old costume fit you, but Al's mom said that was crazy, since you're so much taller than Terrel. So Al's mom stayed up really late and made you a new one."

We climb the stairs backstage and go into a cramped room. Al's mom is waiting there with my brand-new costume: a creamy satin dress with a full, flouncy skirt and a blue ribbon tied around the waist.

"Wow. Thank you!" I say, as I slip it on. "It's really great."

She brushes off my thanks. "No worries, sweetheart," she says, zipping me up. "There. Let me take a look."

She stands back and evaluates, head tilted to one side. "It could be a teensy bit shorter, but I'll take care of that after rehearsal. Everything else looks spot-on. Can you move okay?"

I spin. The skirt of the dress flies out, then floats gracefully down again.

"Arms?" she asks.

I lift my arms overhead.

"Excellent!" she says with satisfaction. "Do I rock, or what?"

"You definitely rock," I reply.

In the meantime, Jessica has slipped her costume on. "We should go," she says. "The others are waiting in one of the studios. We want to run through the dance one more time before rehearsal starts."

"Wait," Al's mom says. "I need to clip a few loose threads."

I can see that Jessica's getting antsy. "Go ahead," I say. "Tell them I'll be there in a minute."

After Al's mom snips the threads, I race out the door and down the stairs. For a moment I'm lost. I don't know how to get to the rehearsal studios from backstage. So I run out onstage, figuring I can find my way if I go through the theater.

Where, it turns out, Mr. Lester and Mr. Tonetti are sitting.

CHAPTER
19

I FREEZE, RIGHT THERE IN THE MIDDLE OF THE STAGE.

Mr. Lester and Mr. Tonetti look up from their seats in the front row.

I'm tempted to run back the way I came and hope they didn't notice anything. But since we're the only three people in the theater and the stage is lit up as bright as day, this seems rather unlikely.

"Um...hi," I say.

They don't say anything.

But they haven't told me to go home yet, so maybe they really have given me a second chance.

And rather than running away like I want to, maybe I need to act like I deserved that chance.

So I walk slowly off the stage and into the audience. Right to where they're sitting.

"Hi," Mr. Lester says.

Mr. Tonetti just squints at me from behind his glasses.

I take a deep breath. "I'd like to thank you both for giving me another chance," I say. "It really means a lot to me. And I won't let you down. I promise."

Mr. Lester nods. "You're welcome, Epatha."

Mr. Tonetti continues to squint at me in silence. Finally he says, "You will do what you are supposed to?" he says. "Because I was not so sure about this another-chance business. This is a favor to Linc Simmons. Not to you."

I start to feel angry—but why *would* Mr. Tonetti trust me? I haven't given him any reason to. Yet.

"I will do what I'm supposed to," I say. "I understand now about how you need to respect the choreographer. And how making things up causes problems and stuff."

Mr. Tonetti does not look convinced.

"We're counting on you, Epatha," Mr. Lester says. "Linc is, too."

"I know," I say. "Thank you again."

"You'd better get going," Mr. Lester says.

Mr. Tonetti grunts.

I run out of the theater and join my friends.

After the encounter with Mr. Lester and Mr. Tonetti, the rest of the rehearsal is a piece of cake. We have to wait while some last-minute lighting changes are made. I see Linc's friend Mac up on the catwalk near the ceiling, moving lights around. Then we run through the ballet without stopping, exactly the way we'll do it for the opening tomorrow night.

Brenda, who dances beside me in the group, makes sure I start off in the right spot, since I've never practiced this dance onstage. But after that, I don't need any help at all. I dance in perfect unison with my friends, just like I promised. Just like I *want* to.

"You did good," JoAnn says, when we're offstage.

"Yeah," Al adds. "No one would ever know you'd just learned a new part."

"Thanks." I grin.

Since we won't get to watch the real performances, we're allowed to sit in the audience tonight after our part's over. We grab front-row seats. The dancers are all graceful and powerful, especially Linc. And it's cool to be sitting close enough to see the sweat on his face and to see him breathing hard. That's what ballet is about: working hard and making it look easy. Now I want to be a professional dancer more than ever.

After the rehearsal is over, the dancers—including us!—gather onstage. Mr. Lester gives us notes, while Mr. Tonetti stands by his side.

"Robert," Mr. Lester says to a tall blond man, "a little slow on your second entrance. And Maribelle, make that last spin sharper, if you can."

As he continues, I can't help it—my eyes drift over to Mr. Tonetti. He's looking right at me. And I think he sees the question in my eyes: *Do you think I did okay?* Because as he holds my gaze, he nods his head, just once.

But that's enough for me. I'm totally, completely, perfectly happy.

CHAPTER
20

IT'S THE BIG NIGHT: SATURDAY NIGHT, THE PREMIERE OF *Springtime in Harlem*. I'm so excited I can hardly hold still. After thinking I'd never dance at the Harlem Ballet, getting this second chance is the best thing ever.

I have to be at the theater at seven o'clock, so I can get into my costume and get my makeup done. Makeup! This really *is* the big time.

Dad drops me off in front of the theater. "Break a leg!" he says, kissing the top of my head. "I know you'll make us all proud."

My friends are just going in the front door. I run to catch up. We make our way to the dressing rooms and open the one marked GIRLS. Our eyes widen as we look around. There's a big, long mirror along the wall with a long makeup table under it. A row of lightbulbs surrounds the mirror.

Ruby, the makeup lady, is waiting to help us get ready. She covers our faces, one by one, with a layer of base, then lines our eyes and paints our lips.

JoAnn looks into the mirror, horrified, after her makeup's done. "We're supposed to be girls! Not clowns!"

Ruby laughs. "The stage lights are bright, dear. You'll look totally normal onstage, believe it or not."

"Not," JoAnn mutters. But Jerzey Mae is thrilled about her makeup. She keeps sneaking glances at herself in the mirror.

Next, a woman named Anna comes to help us into our costumes. "Be very careful," she cautions us. "You don't want to get that makeup on these lovely dresses."

"Curtain in fifteen minutes." The stage manager's voice booms through a speaker hanging in a corner. There's so much excitement in the room

I wouldn't be surprised if we all started floating or bouncing off the walls.

There's a knock on the door. Linc pops his head in. "Good luck, girls," he says. "You, too," we call out in unison. Just before he leaves, he catches my eye and winks.

Almost before we know it, music starts playing. There's a little TV in the dressing room that shows what's happening onstage.

We see the curtains part and Linc spring onto the stage for the first scene.

"Girls to stage left. You're on in five minutes," we hear through the speaker.

Anna leads us down a hallway and quietly opens a door. We pass through heavy black curtains, and all of a sudden, there we are, standing in the wings. We have a side view of Linc doing his solo dance. He finishes, and the stage goes dark.

"You're on!" Anna says.

We walk onto the stage and take our positions for the beginning of the scene. I peek into the audience. It's a little hard to see, but it looks like the theater's full. Then the music begins, light floods the stage, and we're dancing.

We move as a unit, all seven of us together. Linc dances on from stage left. He takes Terrel's hand, and they dance together as the rest of us continue with our steps. The music fills my heart, my soul, my body, and I dance the best I've ever danced, even though I'm doing exactly the steps I'm supposed to do. It's a good thing that smiling is part of the choreography. I think the smiles we have plastered all over our faces are going to last a very long time.

Before we know it, we're back offstage.

We watch the rest of the ballet on the little TV in our dressing room. There's one scene where Linc is supposed to be angry. He flails around and dances like a crazy man. But he always lands right where the spotlight shines on him.

"Everyone, prepare for curtain call," the stage manager says through the speaker, right before the show ends. We wait in the wings until the music stops, and everyone starts clapping. My friends and I run onstage holding hands, and we curtsy. Terrel steps in front and takes a solo bow. A teensy part of me is jealous—but I will have plenty of time later to be a big star.

The applause is deafening. All the other dancers come onstage. Linc takes a solo bow, and then we all bow together. Someone hands

Linc a huge bouquet of roses. After he bows again, he comes over to us. He pulls out seven roses and hands one to each of us. The audience cheers and claps even louder.

Finally, the curtain falls.

CHAPTER
21

AFTERWARD, THERE'S A PARTY IN THE LOBBY. WE'RE ALLOWED to come out in our costumes, although Anna says, "Please, don't spill any juice on them, okay? Please?"

Food is set up on one side of the lobby, and drinks on the other. The place is packed. Jazz music fills the air, and everyone seems really happy.

"My girls!" Ms. Debbé comes over. She's wearing an extra-fancy turban for the occasion, one with blue feathers, and her neck seems to drip with blue jewels. "I am so proud of you. Of all of you," she says, giving each of us a hug in turn.

Mr. Lester is a few steps behind her. "Yes, great

job, girls," he says. "Mr. Tonetti is very impressed. He's even talking about doing another ballet here next year, with more parts for young dancers."

Our families swoop over in a mob. Brenda's mom, Al's mom, the triplets' parents, Terrel's dad and his girlfriend, and my whole family. "*Fantastico!*" Nonna says, kissing my cheeks.

"*¡Fabuloso!*" says Abuela.

All their friends hug me, and so do Mom and Dad. I don't think I've ever been hugged so much in my life.

Even though it's crowded, some people have started dancing to the music. The sea of people parts, and Linc appears. He comes straight over to me.

"May I have this dance?" he asks.

My knees feel like they're going to buckle underneath me. Nonna and Abuela and their friends all have matching expressions: eyes wide and jaws slack.

Linc grabs my hand. "Come on," he says; then he drops his voice. "You told your family you were going to dance with me, right? I don't want to make a liar out of you."

Okay—I know I'm way too young to think about getting married. But when I get old enough, Linc Simmons is gonna be at the top of my list.

He pulls me over to a clear spot, and we start dancing—dancing however we want. He jumps in the air. I jump higher. I've never been so happy. Then I remember exactly why I am where I am tonight.

"Just a sec," I yell over the music. I run back and grab Terrel's hand. She grabs Al, who grabs JoAnn, who grabs Jerzey Mae, who grabs Brenda, who grabs Jessica. I drag the whole line back to Linc, and we dance together in one big, crazy circle. My mom and Abuela join in, and soon, everyone, even Nonna, is dancing with us.

"You are one lucky girl to have such good friends," Linc says as I twirl under his arms.

And you know what? He's right.

Epatha's Guide to Ballet Terms
(With help from Terrel)

battement tendu—a move where you slide your foot on the floor and point your toe. If you want, instead of moving your foot in a straight line, you can swirl it around in little curlicues. No, actually, you can't.

châiné turns—turns that move in one direction across the floor. In a straight line, not little curlicues, in case you were wondering.

demi-plié—a small knee-bend, where you keep your heels on the floor. I like to add fluttery arm swoops when I do these. However, you're not supposed to.

diva—a big star. Like Terrel was in this show. Thank you. But even if you say nice things about me, I'm still going to make sure you get these terms right.

grand plié—a bigger knee-bend. Some people do big, superfancy arm swoops with these. Again, you're not supposed to.

improvise—to make up things, like dance moves, right on the spot. Right, Terrel? I wouldn't know. The idea of making things up on the spot gives me a headache.

jeté—leap. Got a problem with that, T.? No, that's correct. And by the way, you asked me to help you with these definitions!

mantecaditos—Puerto Rican butter cookies, which are very tasty. At least we agree about this. But, they're not really related to ballet.

pirouette—a fancy turn on one leg. A very good diva move. Epatha is particularly good at these, I have to say.

Aw, thanks, Terrel! ☺

Simmons, Linc—a very talented ballet dancer. Who is also very cute. Eww, yuck!

About the Creators

Whoopi Goldberg is the author of the Sugar Plum Ballerinas books. She has won a Tony, an Emmy, an Oscar, and a Grammy, as well as two Golden Globes. In 2001, she was awarded the prestigious Mark Twain Prize for American Humor. She has appeared in scores of films and in all media.

Deborah Underwood is the author of numerous picture books, including *Finding Kindness, Interstellar Cinderella, Part-time Princess*, and the *New York Times* bestsellers *Here Comes the Easter Cat, The Quiet Book*, and *The Loud Book!* Her ballet career was cut short by a tragic lack of talent, but she can sing a mean aria and knows four ukulele chords.

Ashley Evans loves creating colorful, fun, and dynamic art. Born and raised in Queens, she now lives in Charlotte, North Carolina, with her boyfriend and their daughter. When she's not creating art, you can find her decorating cakes, enjoying her family, or catching a much-needed nap!